where is Pidge?

Written & Created by **Michelle Staubach Grimes**

Illustrated by **Bill DeOre**

Pidge Media LLC | whereispidge.com

Publisher's Cataloging-in-Publication

    Grimes, Michelle Staubach.
        Where is Pidge? / written and created by Michelle Staubach Grimes ; illustrated by Bill DeOre.
        pages cm
        SUMMARY: Pidge, a middle child of seven siblings, is angry with her family after being left behind at a restaurant.
        In an attempt to run away, she gets stuck in the laundry chute. After a long day, she is reunited with her family.
        Audience: Ages 4-8.
        LCCN 2014960240
        ISBN 978-0-9908420-0-2

        1. Middle-born children--Juvenile fiction. 2. Families--Juvenile fiction. [1. Middle-born children--Fiction. 2. Families--Fiction.]
        I. DeOre, Bill, illustrator. II. Title.

    PZ7.1.G75Whe 2015

The illustrations in this book are rendered in pencil, pen, ink and watercolor. Typography/font Bodoni and Century Schoolbook.
10 9 8 7 6 5 4 3 2 1 Printed in Canada. First Printing, February 2015.

For **Mom and Dad**

Mom, the real Pidge,
thank you for your
selfless mothering and
commitment to our family,
and Dad, thank you for
your unconditional love.

Love,
Michelle

Pidge sat at the table,
waiting and reading.
She'd been left behind –
but at least she had a book.

Who forgets their kid?

thought Pidge.
A family with too
many kids, that's who.

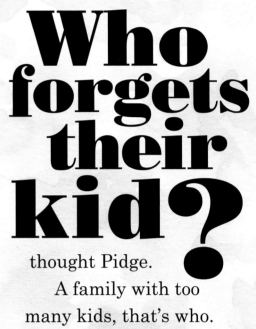

"Oh Pidge, I'm so sorry!"
said Mom, rushing back
into the restaurant.
"Daddy thought you were
in my car, and I thought
you were in his car."

At home, Pidge
headed straight upstairs.
"Same ol' story.
Nobody ever forgets
big kids or babies.
It's just the one
in the middle who
doesn't matter,"
she grumbled.

THUP
THUMP
THUMP
THUMP

Pidge tripped over Maverick and tumbled into her room.
She stepped on Little Petey's cleats as she climbed into bed.
Ouch!
Neither Maverick nor Little Petey budged.
"I get forgotten at a restaurant and now everyone's forgotten this is my room."

In the morning,
    Pidge's room was quiet.
She peeked out her door –
    no one in the hallway.
    She could hear her
family downstairs,
    busy and together.
"If they're gonna forget me,
    then forget them!
I'm running away!"

"I'll slide down the laundry chute and
sneak out the backdoor.
No one will even see me leave."

Yeeeeeeeeeeeeeeeeeeeeeeeeeeee

But Pidge didn't slide
    all the way through
    the chute as planned.

She landed, hard, on
    Michael's football pads.

And before she could figure out what to do next, Katrina's ballet skirt floated down.

SSSwoooooooshhhh
pl0p
darkness

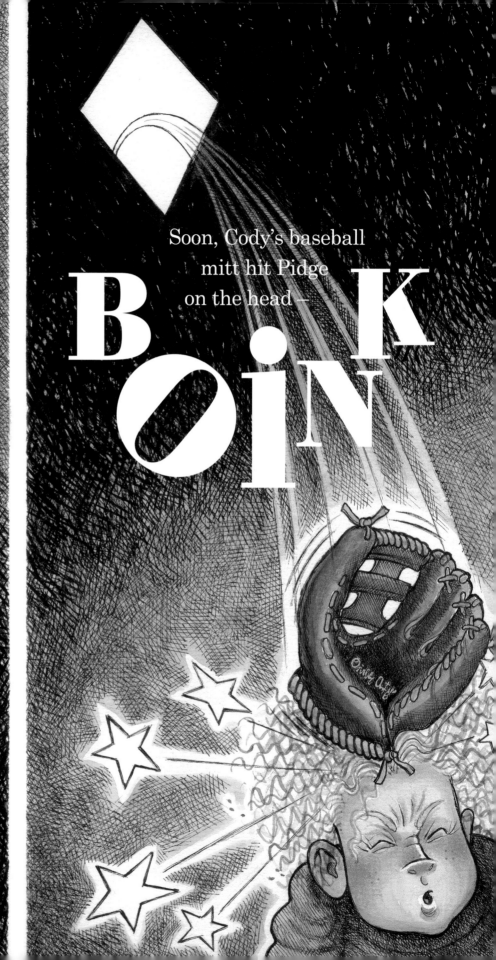

Soon, Cody's baseball mitt hit Pidge on the head—

BOiNK

– followed by Drew's basketball shoe. Later came Lucy's blankie and lots of clothes and towels.

ker-plop
wooooossSShhhh
ploop
ploOf

This was not good! Except...
Pidge found a bag of candy
inside that last pair of pants.

yayYummm
uummm

Being stuck isn't so bad
after all, thought Pidge.
No one can tell me what to do.

Pidge ate.
  And ate.
She hummed.
  She even
napped a little.

hhuummmmmmmmmm

yyyuuuuuuuuuu

A stomachache
woke her up.
Her heart
hurt a little.
And she shivered.

Maybe I miss my family,

Pidge thought.

She pulled on Michael's
football jersey. She slipped on
Katrina's ballet skirt.
She wrapped Lucy's blankie
around her shoulders.

BBrrr
BBrrrr
BrRrrr
rrr
rr

Drew's shoe
warmed one foot.

She rested her head on Cody's baseball mitt. Tears trickled down her cheeks. Pidge was

Stuck in the middle of upstairs and downstairs,
inside and outside, and all of this stuff.

Just then, Pidge
heard Maverick's paws
scrape the laundry room floor.
"Maverick!"
Pidge called.

Pidge wiggled a leg through
the jeans and skirts and football
pads and nudged the laundry
chute door with her big toe.

ruff
rr u
rruff
r u ff
ru fff

Maverick went wild.

And then Pidge heard Mom. "Maverick, what are you doing? Stop scratching!" Maverick barked louder and scratched harder. **"And where IS your buddy Pidge?** We've looked everywhere!"

They're looking for **me,** realized Pidge.

Everyone pounded into
the laundry room to see
why Maverick was
making such a racket.
Just then the
door popped open.
There was Pidge's foot.

**"Help,
pleeease."**

There was Pidge's voice.

Maverick tugged
at the laundry.
There was Pidge!

"Why were you hiding from us?" asked Dad.
"I hate being the middle child," Pidge said.
"I hate being forgotten."
Dad smiled and said,
"Ohhhhhhhhh Pidge.
You're unforgettable!"

The family followed
Pidge to the kitchen table.
  In between bites,
Pidge told them about
  her time in the chute.
When she was done,
  the entire Hoobler family
started talking at once.
  "You think your day
was bad," said Michael.
    "It was worse for us!"
  "We were sad without you,"
    Little Petey said.

"Michael's football practice was boring without your jokes."

"Katrina couldn't decide what to wear."

"Lucy couldn't nap without you reading her to sleep."

"Drew's friends missed your homemade cookies."

"Cody struck out because you weren't cheering from the stands."

STRIKE 3

When the stories stopped, Maverick barked.

"And Maverick's starving," said Dad.

"Pidge," Mom said. "Without you in the middle, we fall apart!"

"Being in the middle means there are people on all sides to love you," Dad said.

By the time the dinner dishes were cleared, Pidge was starting to think they might be right. She looked down and said,

"Mav, I'll never try to wiggle out of the middle again."

Pictured here is the author's mother, Marianne Hoobler Staubach, with her dad, George William Hoobler. Grandpa Hoobler called Marianne his "Little Pigeon," which later evolved into her nickname, **"Pidge."** The story of the real Pidge Hoobler began in Cincinnati, Ohio, in 1942.

To my editor,
Liz Garton Scanlon,
thank you for believing in me,
sharing your wisdom and your
relentless support.

To my illustrator,
Bill DeOre, thank you for
listening to my vision, never doubting
me and bringing Pidge to life with your
beautiful illustrations. I'm eternally
grateful to you.

XO,
Michelle